In memory of my grandmother,
Beatrice Evelyn Harvey (née Bairstowe)
1883–1972

Clarion Books
a Houghton Mifflin Company imprint
215 Park Avenue South, New York, NY 10003
Copyright © 2004 by Jan Ormerod
First published in Australia in 2004 by Little Hare Books.
First American edition, 2005.

The illustrations were executed in watercolors.
The text was set in 18-point Cochin.

www.houghtonmifflinbooks.com

Library of Congress Cataloging-in-Publication Data
Ormerod, Jan.
Lizzie nonsense / by Jan Ormerod.
p. cm.
Summary: Her mother calls it nonsense when Lizzie pretends that their house is pretty or that
a bath is the sea, but it turns out that imagination runs in the family.
ISBN 0-618-57493-X
[1. Imagination–Fiction. 2. Australia–Fiction.] I. Title.
PZ7.O634Li 2005
[E]–dc22
2004026642

ISBN-13: 978-0-618-57493-3
ISBN-10: 0-618-57493-X
Printed in Hong Kong

10   9   8   7   6   5   4   3   2   1

Lizzie Nonsense

JAN ORMEROD

CLARION BOOKS ❧ NEW YORK

When Lizzie's mama and papa were married, the sun shone on fields of yellow wheat that grew right up to the door of the tiny church. But for as long as Lizzie can remember, she and Mama and Papa and baby have lived in their little house in the bush, and the church and neighbors are far away.

When Papa takes the sandalwood that he has cut into town, it is fifty miles along sand tracks, and he is away a long time.

Then Lizzie and Mama and baby are all alone in the little house in the bush.

Lizzie is always playing and pretending.
She is always dreaming.

"Lizzie nonsense!" her mama calls it.

Every morning, Lizzie and Mama carry water from the creek for the vegetable patch and for baby's bath.

Lizzie blows bubbles to make baby laugh.
"You're afloat in a boat on a big, wide sea," she sings.
"You and your nonsense!" says her mama.

Then Lizzie picks flowers while Mama tends the garden.

"I'm a bride," says Lizzie. "Look at my beautiful bouquet."
"What a lot of nonsense!" says her mama. "Brides carry roses."

There is always work to be done inside the house, too.

While Mama scrubs the table, Lizzie says,
"This house is as pretty as a picture."
"Lizzie," says her mama, "you are full of nonsense."

Sometimes a snake crawls in and goes to sleep under the rug.
Lizzie and baby must sit on the table until Mama has chased it out.

"You're the bravest mama in the world!" says Lizzie.
"Nonsense!" says Mama.

In the evening, Lizzie helps Mama prepare dinner.

"Tonight," says Lizzie, "we will eat peaches,
and cream, and little sweet cakes."
"Such nonsense!" says her mama. "We are having
turnips, as usual."

After dinner, when baby is asleep,
there is usually some mending to be done.

"I am making a party dress with lots of frills
and lace and bows," says Lizzie.
"What an imagination," says her mama.

But Lizzie's mama likes to imagine, too. Every Sunday, they put on their best clothes and put baby in his carriage. Then they walk along the track and back, and Mama pretends they have been to church.

Lizzie and her mama wish that the dingoes
howling outside at night were imaginary.

"I'm going to sleep in your bed to keep you safe," says Lizzie.

Finally one morning, after many weeks have passed,
Lizzie cries, "What do I see? Is that a dust cloud from
my papa's team of horses?"
"Nonsense!" says her mama. "It's your head that
is in the clouds."

"But is my imagination playing tricks as well?"
Mama wonders aloud. "I can hear harnesses jangling
and the dog barking. Make haste, Lizzie, make haste!"

Mama picks up baby, and they run helter-skelter down the
track toward Papa and the horses.

Papa lifts Lizzie high into the air and sits her on Bessie's broad back. Then he takes Mama in his arms.

"You are as pretty as a picture, Beatrice," he says. "Pretty as the day we were married, you with your white dress and bouquet of yellow roses."

"Nonsense, Albert!" says Mama.

"And you," he says to Lizzie, "are as brave and pretty as your mother."

"Nonsense!" says Lizzie.

And together they walk back to their little house in the bush.